PAX & PETEE'S PLAYGROUND ADVENTURE

WRITTEN BY

TRINA C. BASS

Illustrations By

Sean Randolph

Great morning to you!

This day will be the brightest 'tis true.

Staying focused hooray!

Watching every word that I say!

Pax and Petee recited this phrase every morning and evening.

The goal was to ensure they had the best day dreaming.

That was actually pretty cleaver for a sister and a brother.

They loved to have fun and play games with one another.

Away they went on their journey to play.

This time on the playground just a few blocks away.

Their imagination took them so far.

Starting with the monkey bars that took them to Mars.

Pax and Petee ran without a stop.

Climbing the monkey bars, swinging and twisting all the way to the top. "We're headed to Mars," Petee screamed and shouted! "Wait for me! Wait for me," Pax grinned and pouted.

In their minds they had now become astronauts.

Running, tripping, and falling over a barrel of apricots.

Racing to climb into the awaiting space shuttle.

Their movement was swift and not very subtle.

Heading to the fourth planet from the sun.

The second smallest reddish one from which the Solar System begun.

"We made it! We made it!" They cheered so happily you see.

After bouncing around in zero gravity feeling very free.

Pax and Petee were now headed to the swings.

Flying had now become next on their list of real things.

The swings were fun as they went higher and higher.

Feeling like they were flying as they opened their eyes in their navigator attire.

"I'm flying this airplane so make sure to buckle your seatbelt," said Pax.

"We are headed for the hills, this should be a great thrill," screamed Petee. Through the skies they went flying higher and higher.

Now it's time to land, these two pilots must retire.

The hills were Pax and Petee's favorite.

They could imagine two things at once and savor it.

Climbing the hills felt like mountains so high.

Up and down the high hills they went with joy and a sigh.

Touching the clouds was such a thrill.

Sliding after climbing was next after this venture was fulfilled.

Heading for the Grand Canyon was their sole intent.

Viewing the beautiful sights felt like minutes well spent.

The trees they were both climbing without a fright so high.

The climb made them feel like birds in the sky.

Resting on each branch for their next journey to try.

The slide felt like a magical rollercoaster ride.

The ups and downs were opposite of the merry-go-round.

Around and around and around they go.

The very first stop only Pax and Petee will know.

"The ships straight ahead and I think I see a small city," Petee said.

After minutes of riding they both became very dizzy.

Feeling seasick had now become such a great pity.

The balance beams and planks were their next mission to try.

Dreaming of the Olympics for a gold medal you can't buy.

The playhouse was the next and closest in distance.

To them it felt like a beautiful mansion filled with buttermilk biscuits.

This amazing mansion was filled so high with burgers, pizza, and spaghetti to try.

Candy was piled in each and every room.

Their teeth was sure to meet a very aching dome.

Next in sight was a tunnel you see.

Leading to the train tracks was certainly meant to be.

On the railroad train they went so fast.

Riding through town after town they nearly ran out of gas.

The sea-saw was their last playground ride to tour.

With one on each side this should be a chore.

The sea-saw felt like a galloping horse.

With cowboy hats, a farm, and some long ropes of course.

Up and down again Pax and Petee surely went.

What a great day at the playground for a day well spent.

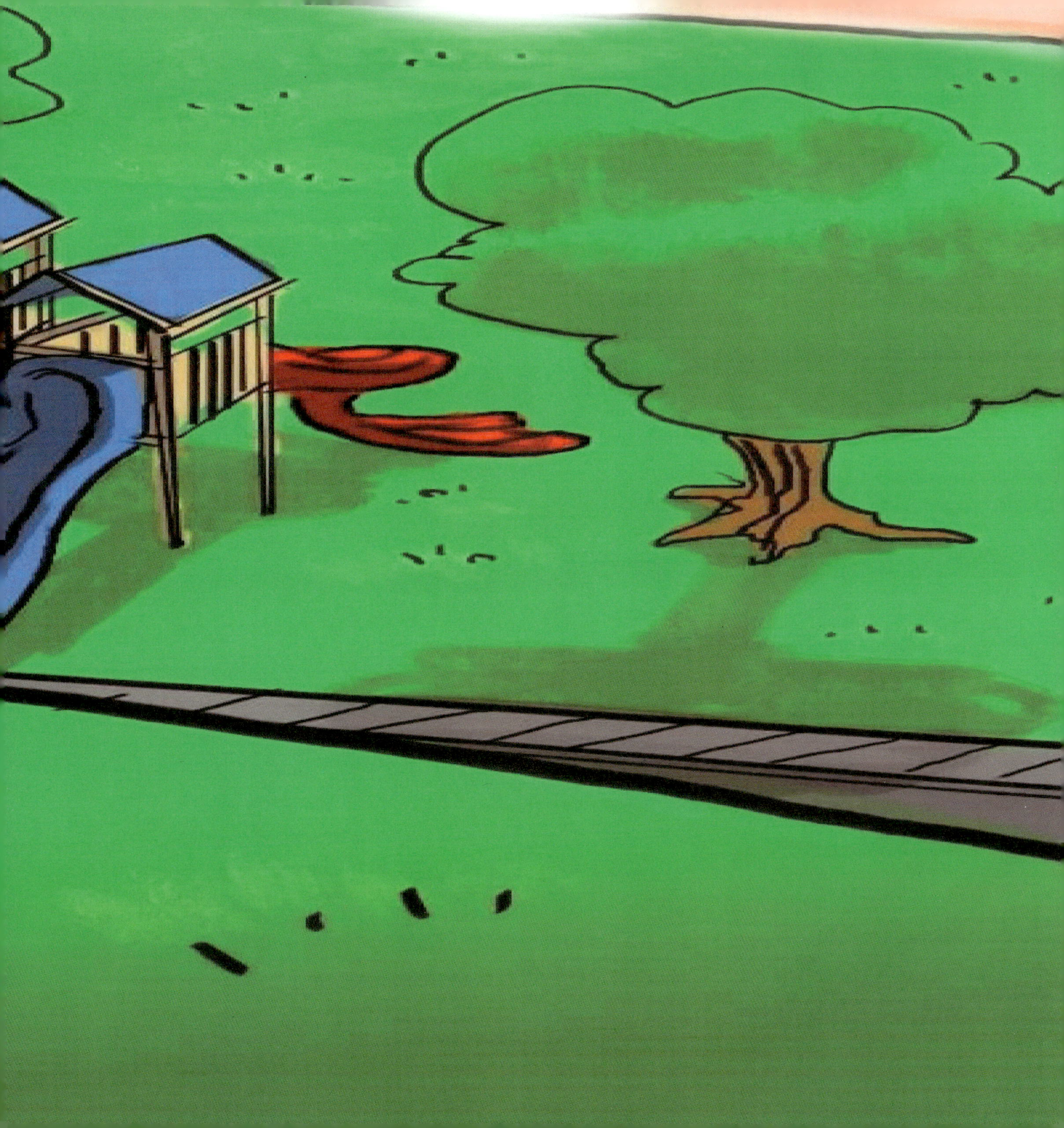

FUN LEARNING ACTIVITIES
For
PAX & PETEE'S
Playground Adventure

1. Unscramble the words
2. Fill in the blank
3. Wacky Word Search
4. Big Word Vocabulary
5. Find the missing letters
6. Multiple choice questions
7. Use your imagination like Pax and Petee to draw your very own picture

<u>UNSCRAMBLE THE WORDS</u>

1. XPA _____

2. TEPEE _____

3. YALPOUNDGR _____

4. NEVURETAD _____

5. ERMAD _____

6. OTHERBR _____

7. ISETSR _____

FILL IN THE BLANK

1. Pax and Petee are brother and _____.

2. Pax and Petee love to have fun at the _____.

3. The _____ were Pax and Petee's favorite.

4. Pax and Petee were headed for the Grand _____.

5. They felt like _____ in the sky.

6. Dreaming of the _____ for a gold medal you can't buy.

7. The slide felt like a magical _____ ride.

WACKY WORD SEARCH

Find the following words:

1. TRAIN
2. DREAM
3. PAX
4. GOLD
5. BIRDS
6. FUN
7. PETEE

E	T	R	A	I	N	C
E	D	K	D	L	O	G
T	R	B	I	R	D	S
E	E	Q	W	T	G	R
P	A	X	E	G	O	Y
V	M	E	H	F	U	N

DISCOVER THE HIDDEN WORD BELOW:

1.__I__ 2.____ 3.__A__ 4.____ 5.__I__ 6.____ 7.____

25

BIG WORD VOCABULARY

1. Define the word navigator?

2. Define the word Solar System?

3. Define the word gravity?

4. Define the word astronaut?

5. Define the word imagination?

6. Define the word recite?

7. Define the word attire?

8. Define the word Grand Canyon?

9. Define the word journey?

10. Define the word Olympics?

Two answers given...

Navigator: a person who directs the route of a ship or aircraft by using instruments or maps.

Solar System: a group of eight planets including their moons in orbit around the sun, including smaller bodies in the form of comets.

FIND THE MISSING LETTERS

1. G_ and Can_on

2. _ly_pics

3. _avi_ator

4. Gra_ity

5. As_rona_t

6. So_ar S_stem

7. Ima_in_tio_

MULTIPLE CHOICE QUESTIONS

1. Pax and Petee went where _____?

    a. to the zoo   **b.** to the playground   **c.** swimming

2. Pax and Petee are _____?

    a. pigs   **b.** monkeys   **c.** dogs

3. Pax and Petee love to _____?

    a. day dream   **b.** eat ice cream   **c.** stay home

4. Pax and Petee were dreaming of the Olympics to win a _____?

    a. bike   **b.** toy   **c.** gold medal

USE YOUR IMAGINATION LIKE PAX AND PETEE TO DRAW YOUR VERY OWN PICTURE

Made in the USA
Columbia, SC
26 January 2018